Messiah

THE LITTLE-KNOWN STORY OF
HANDEL'S BELOVED ORATORIO

Tim Slover

SILVERLEAF
PRESS

Author's note: When quoting Eighteenth Century documents, I have preserved contemporary spelling, capitalization, and punctuation. It is hoped by this that the reader will catch the spirit of the time—and, upon reflection, gain a greater appreciation for English teachers.

A New Sacred Oratorio

It is the Lenten season in London, 1743, the night of March 23, and the theater-going public is in chastened mood. No plays, no operas—in fact, no secular entertainments of any kind—seem appropriate now, and indeed, it is hard to find them during this forty-day season of penance and reflection before the gladness of Easter. But at the Theatre Royal, Covent Garden, a modern, elegant palace of entertainment in its eighth year of existence under the management of John Rich, the curtain is about to go up on a new work altogether appropriate to the season.

Or is it appropriate? It is by George Frederick Handel, celebrated composer of church music—but also of secular operas. Into which category will this new entertainmnet fall? Perhaps into both, for it is one of his hybrid oratorios. For reasons known best to himself, he has chosen to veil its title: all the notices advertise it simply as *A New Sacred Oratorio*. Ominously, some of those notices have been torn down. And, contrary to the usual practice, the word book is not readily available. What can that signify?

Inside the theater, one cannot help but

Theatre Royal, Covenant Garden, 1808

be impressed. Covent Garden is lavish. Rich has spent the money earned by the theatre's first hit, John Gay's *Beggar's Opera*, on beautiful fittings. (Appropriate to this age of pithy aphorisms that unprecedented success yielded the happy quip, "*The Beggar's Opera* made Gay rich, and Rich gay.") Four tiers of boxes, each lit by a dozen crystal chandeliers, surround an extensive pit, all gleaming in cream and gold.

Certainly the stage is in chastened attire. No scenery as one would normally see at an opera, of course. But usually, behind the proscenium arch on the raised, raked platform, one sees a splendid organ when one of Mr. Handel's oratorios is performing. Indeed, he often favors his audiences by playing during the intervals. Now there is only a simple harpsichord. And the company of instrumentalists seems small—just some strings and timpani, an oboe or two, a bassoon, and perhaps a glimpse of a trumpet. When the choir enters it is in force no more than thirty, and not a costume to be seen. Lenten, indeed.

Ah, here comes Matthew Dubourg, the fine violinist and orchestra leader. Although he lives in Ireland, honored with the post of Master and Composer of State Music, he has often come to London to serve as concert-master for Handel. As they watch Dubourg tune the orchestra some in the audience smile, having heard the rumor of a memorable night last winter in Dublin when he took flight on a particularly long, improvised cadenza of his own devising. When at last he returned to the notes on the page,

Handel is said to have growled so that all could hear him to the very last row, "You are welcome home, Mr. Dubourg!"

Now the vocal soloists enter from the wings to a ripple of applause and sit at the very front of the stage, and one cannot suppress a tremor of excitement. Handel has selected them, as always, for their ability to sight-read and assimilate new material quickly and, as much, for their willingness to subjugate ego to the demands of the music and text. There is the reliable tenor John Beard, veteran of many Handel entertainments, who sings with such wonderful dignity and expression. He was a soloist in Handel's very first oratorio, *Esther*, eleven years ago and has sung many lead parts

Drury Lane Theatre, 1775

since. Just last week he sang the title role of Handel's other new oratorio for the season, *Samson*, to great acclaim. But tonight he sings no title role because in this *New Sacred Oratorio*, it is rumored, there are no named parts, no traditional dramatic story line to follow.

Sitting beside Mr. Beard is the other tenor, the new man from Drury Lane Theatre, Thomas Lowe, a singer who, while reputed to be somewhat limited in versatility, is known to possess a powerful and thrilling voice. And there is Signora Christina Avolio, a soprano of consummate professionalism and the last of the Italian stars from his opera days. And there, on the other side, another newcomer, the German bass, Henry Theodore Reinhold.

But if the eye passes with pleasure over these fine singers, it is riveted by the two famous—or infamous—women coming on stage now. Horace Walpole, writer and politician, recently dismissed them

Mrs. Catherine "Kitty" Clive

Mr. Theophilus Cibber

Mrs. Susannah Cibber

derisively as "goddesses from the farces." They are Mrs. Catherine "Kitty" Clive and Mrs. Susannah Cibber, and they are a study in contrasts. Kitty is buxom, lively and pert, with a high, sugary soprano voice and mercurial personality which can by turns be coquettish, and then, in a flash, as catty as her nickname. Susannah is slight, grave, uncommonly pale, with an aristocratic nose and large, expressive brown eyes. The two women dislike each other as much as it is possible to do and remain on the same stage together.

Most in the audience know they were rivals for years at Drury Lane Theatre just down the road. A war grew up between them, created and inflamed by Susannah's hateful husband Theophilus—some-time actor-manager at Drury Lane, full-time gambler, drinker, and carouser. He it was who demanded in the newspapers that Kitty surrender her most beloved role, Polly in *The Beggar's Opera*, to his young wife—not because Susannah wanted the part, but because by playing it, she would earn more money to hand over to him. When Kitty publicly accused the Cibbers of trying to ruin her, the Polly War began, each side and its supporters firing volleys in print at each other.

The war was never resolved; rather a more salacious scandal overwhelmed it, one which drove Susannah from the theater. For five years she had not set foot upon a London stage, until last week, when she sang the role of Micah in *Samson*. Those close to the front of the theater can see that she looks stricken. And Mr. Beard looks unwell. Why?

But these speculations cease when the composer, himself, barges onto the Covent Garden stage in his usual hurried, ungainly fashion. He has waited until Mr. Dubourg has thoroughly tuned the orchestra, as he cannot abide the sound, but now here he is, the unrivalled musical master of the town, the composer of forty operas, a dozen oratorios, and the very anthems to which the Hanoverian Kings of England are crowned and their royal children wedded: George Frederick Handel. Years before he adopted the English spelling of his name, a signification that, though a German from Halle and a frequent visitor to the Continent to acquire singers, he is English now, Mr. Handel of London.

In public, Handel prefers the old-fashioned full-bottomed wig over the lighter ones just coming into fashion; it better suits his large, portly frame. Charles Burney, his first biographer, who knew him

Handel, Jan van dr Banck, 1711 ca.

in life, described his physical appearance thus: "Handel was large, and he was somewhat corpulent, and unwieldy in his motion; but his countenance, which I remember as perfectly as that of any man

I saw but yesterday, was full of ire and dignity; and such as impressed ideas of superiority and genius.... Handel's general look was somewhat heavy and sour; but when he did smile, it was his sire the sun, bursting out of a black cloud. There was a sudden flash of intelligence, wit, and good humour beaming in his countenance, which I hardly saw in any other."

Handel's temperament is by turns placid and fiery. Burney found him "impetuous, rough, and peremptory in his manners and conversations, but totally devoid of ill-nature or malevolence." He is combative with professional rivals, and not always philosophical when his own compositions fail to please. "You are damnable dainty!" he complained to a couple of gentlemen attending one of his popular works. "You would not got to Theodora—there was room enough to dance there, when that was performed." On the other hand, when his friends once lamented the lack of audience at another performance,

Handel pointed out the acoustic advantage of a small house: "Never mind. The music will sound all the better."

Handel's no-nonsense manner with musicians is legendary. He is fluent in five languages and can swear as fluently in all five. Perhaps it is his way of coping with some of the most preening, egotistical personalities of the age. When opera diva Francesca Cuzzoni petulantly refused to sing a particular aria at a rehearsal conducted in the second story-salon of his house on Brook Street, he is reputed to have raged, "Madam, I know you are a veritable devil, but I would have you know that I am Beelzebub, chief of the Devils." He then took her up by the waist and threatened to throw her out the window if she said one more word on the subject.

Almost as famous for his appetite for food and drink as for his music, Handel once excused himself from a party at his own house, claiming to have been struck by inspiration. When a guest later spied him through a keyhole, he discovered the composer sampling a bottle of burgundy. Perhaps recognizing that inspiration comes from many sources, he left the composer in peace.

Tonight Handel wears an anxious expression, and again one cannot help but wonder why.

The knowledgeable in the audience know the identity of the expensively dressed gentleman sitting in a very good

Charles Jennens, *Thomas Hudson, oil on canvas, c.1744. © Handel House Collections Trust.*

seat. He is in possession of one of the few word books of the new oratorio, which he pores over, scowling all the while. This is Charles Jennens, wealthy squire of Gopsal estate in Leicestershire and writer of the libretto for tonight's entertainment. Mr. Jennens is talented both as writer and musician—he wrote the libretto for Handel's *Saul*, contributed a poem at Handel's request to the oratorio, *L'Allegro, Il Penseroso, ed Il Moderato*, and probably compiled the scripture collection which became the text for *Israel in Egypt*. (As that recent oratorio did not succeed, he does not acknowledge himself its librettist.)

Jennens is part of that small, curious tribe in Georgian England known as "non-jurors," individuals caught between two worlds: they will not sign the loyalty oath to the House of Hanover because they believe its reign to be illegitimate, but being staunch Anglicans, neither will they support the claims of the Catholic Jacobites who wish to restore the Stuart line of James II. A hundred years earlier such a political position might have cost Jennens his life. In these more tolerant times, when the monarchy is becoming more and more a figurehead, it simply means he cannot hold public office. Without a seat in the House of Lords, or the duties of a magistrate to attend to, he is free to pursue his passion—sacred music for the stage.

But why does Mr. Jennens look so angry and unhappy at the premiere of his own work? The mystery of tonight's performance deepens.

On stage, all the instrumentalists and singers in place,

King George II

Handel sits at the harpsichord ready to signal Dubourg to begin the overture. But instead of giving the downbeat, Handel's attention is drawn out into the second tier of boxes. He stands and bows deeply.

All turn in their seats to follow Handel's gaze. There, just taking his place in the royal box, is the King! This is deeply surprising and as deeply gratifying to the ardent Handelians in the audience. The King had been Handel's loyal patron in the years when his beloved Queen Caroline was alive, but it has been four years since he has attended any performance of Handel's music. What can have brought His Majesty to Covent Garden Theatre tonight?

If one is in the front of the pit, gazing back into the house provides a bewildering study in contrasts: the splendid sight of George II, once again gracing the royal box, but also a disconcerting view of many empty seats. Covent Garden Theatre can comfortably hold over eighteen hundred souls, but tonight only a fraction of that number is in attendance. Something has kept them away.

A worried composer, soloists anxious or indisposed, an angry librettist, a rare appearance by the King, a half-filled house, and an oddly ambiguous title for tonight's entertainment: these are the mysteries swirling around the Theatre Royal, Covent Garden this early spring evening, the night of the first London performance of Handel's celebrated oratorio, *Messiah*.

To solve these mysteries, we must retrace the path of Handel's history. ❧

Queen Caroline
(1683-1737)

From Opera to Oratorio

As much as any composer who ever lived, Handel's life was defined by his art. There are ghosts in the public record of a romance when he was a young man in Italy and of anonymous women friends in London, but he never married. Perhaps this was because he spent the overwhelming majority of his waking hours working. Certainly his output as a composer was prodigious: forty operas, thirty masques and oratorios, scores of anthems, odes, songs, concerti, and suites.

But composing was only a part of Handel's musical life. Unlike Bach with his sinecure in Leipzig, or Vivaldi with a salary from a girls' school, Handel made his living year after year as a man of business. And his business was the producing, directing, and performing of his own music in public theaters in London. With the aid of his two successive copyists, the father and son John Christopher Smiths, he also published for sale as many of his scores as printer John Walsh would accept.

The Royal Family, fellow Germans from the same region of Hanover, were staunch supporters of his work, but this did not translate into financial security for Handel, as the Crown only sporadically underwrote his opera seasons. When weddings or other occasions called for it, the Hanovers commissioned music from him, but this was never enough to live on, and, anyway, Handel was no court composer. By temperament he was an entrepreneur. He spent several months of every year striking business deals with theater owners, auditioning and hiring singers, and rehearsing and performing instrumental music, operas, and oratorios. His fortunes rose or fell with the public's reception of his music, and there were lean times as well as prosperous ones.

The demands of making music in public

required of Handel a fast-paced but predictably patterned life. During the 1710s, 20s, and 30s when he was composing operas, Handel spent part of every year scouring the Continent for new singers, mostly the Italian sopranos and castrati who were the stars of the Italian operas then in vogue in London. (As oratorios began to fill more of his repertoire, he turned to England to find most of his talent.) The bulk of the rest of the year Handel spent in rehearsal and performance. A keyboardist

Harpsichord, from the Permanent Collection belonging to South Kensington Museum. Date about 1590.

without peer (rivaled only by Bach on the Continent), he accompanied all his operas and oratorios himself and often "exerted himself," as he put it, on the organ or harpsichord at the intervals—thus as-

suring audiences of at least one spectacular performance for their money. He also gave instrumental concerts.

This schedule was punishing, particularly to his right arm which had a tendency towards numbness and paralysis, and many summers found him at the spa towns of Bath, Tunbridge Wells, or Aachen, recovering his health by taking the waters.

That left Handel only the late summer to compose. His habit was to write two new major works each year to put into production for the next subscription season. These would play cheek by jowl with revivals and pastiches—those peculiar 18th Century amalgams of arias and choruses from several different musical entertainments combined into one musical variety show. Some have mused on the miraculously short time it took Handel to write the music for *Messiah*, only about three weeks. If such is the case we must extend the miracle to his entire career, for all his music for the theater was written at speed, the necessary habit for someone whose professional life was as full as his.

Handel's habit of deriving his music from the work of other composers is legendary. The practice irritated his *Messiah* collaborator Charles Jennens. After receiving some scores from his friend and constant correspondent, Edward Holdsworth, Jennens wrote, "Handel has borrowed a dozen of the Pieces, & I dare say I shall catch him stealing from them; as I have formerly, both from Scarlatti & Vinci." But Jennens's exasperation tells us more about his

Domenico Scarlatti, *portrayed by Domingo Antonio Velasco, 1736*

status as an amateur musical dabbler with no need to worry about earning an income than it does about Handel's character. It was commonplace and entirely acceptable among professionals in this era to borrow musical themes from one another and revise them for one's own composition. All composers did it and, providing they did not claim another's tune as their own—and Handel never did—no opprobrium attached to them.

Once, when asked why he borrowed so much from the music of Bonancini, Handel is said to have quipped, "It's much too good for him; he did not know what to do with it." And indeed, his versions were invariably superior to the original music upon which he built his themes. Contemporary English composer William Boyce summed up Handel's talent for reworking best: "He takes other men's pebbles and polishes them into diamonds." There was one composer from whom Handel stole more music than any other: himself. He frequently reworked his own tunes and harmonies and found places for them in whatever he happened to be working on at the moment. *Messiah* is no exception.

As a young man, Handel had come to London in the autumn of 1710 from Germany by way of Rome to make his mark as a composer of Italian operas. He succeeded almost immediately; the gentry of the town were champing at the bit to experience this new musical form already popular on the Continent. He wrote Rinaldo in just two weeks and immediately staged it in February of 1711, selling the word book and tickets from White's Coffee House in Chesterfield Street. It was a hit. Noting this, other composers— Porpora, Bonancini—flocked to London to take advantage of Handel's success. But Handel's protean opera company, shifting from theater to theater over the years, adding and subtracting singers and

instrumentalists as needed, managed to stay one step ahead of the competition for two decades.

But then in 1733 a new opera company arose. Called the Opera of the Nobility, the new company effectively diluted the talent needed for fine performances and split the paying audience in half. Handel managed to outlast the Opera of the Nobility—and Lord Middlesex's company which succeeded it—but in the process, Italian opera in London took a palpable hit. Mid-century London's population was about 700,000, one of the largest cities in Europe, but, of course, only a small fraction of that population went to the opera, and it was not enough to support more than one company. And, too, throughout the 1730s London gradually lost its taste for Italian opera. John Gay had given it a sharp elbow in the ribs in 1728 with his hilarious lampoon of the form, the immensely popular *Beggar's Opera*. It never recovered. Londoners turned away from Italian opera and increasingly toward musical entertainments performed in their own tongue by such companies as the English Opera Company.

It is popularly supposed that, seeing Italian opera founder, Handel shrewdly turned his hand to writing oratorios in the late 1730s, but this is not so. He continued writing operas right up to 1741, and his first oratorio, *La Resurrezione* was, in fact written when he was a stripling living in Rome. What is true is that his oratorios, though conforming to the strictures of the form—Biblical subject matter, no staging, sets, or costumes—

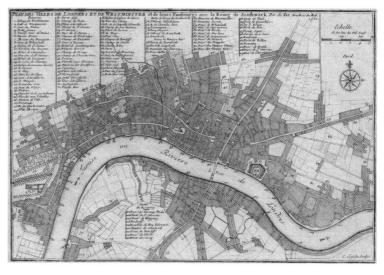

Map of London, *England, by Nicolas de Fer, Paris 1700*

always had a strong operatic flavor. He favored libretti which were dramatic, and he turned the words into tuneful choruses and bravura arias, putting his musical stamp on the form so effectively that he may almost be said to have invented the form, as he had the organ concerto.

Handel's first venture in English oratorios was *Esther*, penned in 1718. In 1732 he revised it and put it on the stage. It was an unexpected success, and Handel followed it up with a second oratorio, *Deborah*, the next season. This was the piece of music which brought him together with the nineteen-year-old Susannah Arne.

He had heard her sing before. Her father and her musical brother, Thomas Arne (the composer of "Rule Britannia"), had launched the English Opera Company that same year and had had the audacity to pirate Handel's classical masque, *Acis and Galatea*, for two performances at his New Theatre, Susannah singing the role of Galatea. Handel was angered by the theft but captivated by Susannah's musical manner.

By all accounts, even the most sympathetic, neither Susannah Arne's voice nor her musicianship was strong. Even Charles Burney, who

Mr. Thomas Arne

admired Susannah, noted that "her voice was a thread and her knowledge of music very inconsiderable." This was a combination calculated to raise ire, not admiration, from Handel. He expected his singers to be note perfect from the first rehearsal, and to sight-read quickly everything set before them. To an unfortunate singer who had represented himself as among that elite group he had once roared, "You scoundrel, did you not tell me you could sing at sight?" "Yes, sir, and so I can," the singer is supposed to have tremulously replied, "but not at first sight." A cathedral singer who came down from Worcester to audition for Handel in London was similarly dismissed: "This is the way you praise God at Worcester?" Handel is said to have asked. "Yes," was the reply. "God is very good, and will no doubt hear your praises at Worcester," Handel rumbled, "but no man will hear them at London." Strictly true or not, these anecdotes underscore what was known to every singer: Mr. Handel accepts no amateurism.

Yet with Susannah Arne, Handel curbed his impatience. Burney notes that something about Susannah's "voice and manner softened Handel's severity at her want of musicianship." He spent long hours with her at the harpsichord, playing a phrase over and over until she had memorized it. To Handel's way of thinking, he was amply rewarded for his pains. Never mind that Miss Arne was a middling contralto. Here was a singer more interested in communicating the drama of a musical role than in showing off, with many a trill and unnaturally extended syllable, the range and power of her voice. As Burney, who idolized Susannah, noted, "from her intelligence of words and native feeling, she sang...in a more touch-

ing manner than the finest opera singer." She had done it as Galatea. She would do it in *Deborah*. And later, she would bring the same sensibility to *Messiah*.

The period from 1738–1741 proved to be tumultuous years for Handel, bringing with them artistic triumphs and financial

Handel

failures. The most prodigious of the setbacks came in the form of operas. *Faramondo* (1738) played eight performances at the King's Theatre, Haymarket, to small and listless houses, and that was the most success any of Handel's last four operas enjoyed. *Serse*, which premiered in April of the same year, closed after only five performances and was never revived in Handel's lifetime. This must have been particularly galling to him, knowing as he would have, that, with its beautiful, gentle larghetto aria, "Ombra mai fu" (better known as "Handel's Largo"), *Serse* was among the very finest of his operatic achievements. The following season, no longer welcome at the Haymarket, Handel produced at Lincoln's Inn Fields Theatre. His operas fared no better there. *Imeneo*, which premiered in November 1740, had only two performances. *Deidamia*, which Handel brought on two months later in January 1741, his fortieth and final opera, faltered after only three. Handel never wrote another opera.

Curiously, these failures at the box office were accompanied by a civic triumph. The town was no longer interested in his operas, but it still delighted to honor him. In 1739, while it was staying away from his music, it erected a statue of him in the Vauxhall pleasure gardens on the outskirts of London, the only living musician to be so honored. In commemoration, John Walsh published Handel's greatest achievement in orchestral music, his Opus 6 concerti, a compostion as grand and ingenious as Bach's Brandenburgs.

Meanwhile, Handel was returning to oratorio. He had found a fine new librettist in Charles Jennens, fifteen years his junior, a man who knew literature as well as music. Jennens had sent him a libretto

King's Theatre, *Haymarket, William Capon*

Vauxhall Gardens, *Samuel Wale, 1751*

its second night when the Royal Family attended, and did moderately well financially, though not enough to salvage Handel's season at the Haymarket that year.

His next two collaborations with Jennens received a mixed reception. The usual format of an oratorio followed that of opera, its story told chiefly through aria and recitative, reserving choral passages for commentary. *Israel in Egypt* (1739), a collection of scriptures put together by Jennens from the Book of Exodus, was a bold departure from this scheme: Handel set it entirely as choruses. The experiment proved too bold for his audience, and the oratorio sputtered out quickly—even after Handel hastily added a few solos for the second

some three years previously. Now Handel returned to it, and discoverd it to be the very sort of dramatic story which lit his creative fires hottest. The oratorio which resulted was *Saul*. Its combination of intelligent words, dramatic incidents, and music of remarkable beauty and fire, make it among the finest achievements in oratorio in any age. Handel wrote the score in the summer of 1738 and premiered it in 1739. A tonic to the tired Italian opera season, it met with "general applause by a numerous and splendid audience" on

Handel Statue, Vauxhall Garden

night in an abortive attempt to salvage it. And in *Israel in Egypt*, Handel's musical borrowing may have gone a step too far. The music he had composed for the Westminster Abbey funeral of Queen Caroline (d. November 22, 1737) he lifted wholesale and made into the first act of the oratorio. The wound was still too fresh in the King's heart; he did not attend *Israel in Egypt*. And he stayed away from Handel's music thereafter. This was ominous to a composer who had always enjoyed royal approval.

Lincoln Inn Field Theatre

At Handel's request, Jennens contributed a poem, "Il Moderato" to his next piece for the theater, a masque setting of two Milton poems, "L'Allegro" and "Il Penseroso." Handel spread the word that, if this musical offering was rejected by the public, there would be consequences. His supporters wrote pieces in the newspapers urging a large opening night attendance. It did not work.

And so the 1740–41 season at Lincoln's Inn Fields Theatre came to its dismal end, cut short by management to avoid further financial hemorrhaging. It was Handel's most disastrous ever, and he talked openly of leaving London permanently and returning to his native Germany. He was fifty-five years old and had lost both his royal patronage and his principal livelihood, Italian opera. The old ache in his arm returned. Perhaps he was played out. Perhaps he should quit music altogether.

And that is where we shall leave him for the moment. It is well to remember that even for prodigies moments of black depression and self-doubt arise, and that even geniuses cannot see the future. ✤

The Cause of a Criminal Conversation

Susannah Arne was the daughter of an ambitious father and the sister of a talented, profligate brother, both named Thomas Arne. Thomas senior, originally by trade an upholsterer and undertaker in the Covent Garden area of London, was the sort of man who took advantage of any angle he could find to advance his fame and fortune. And when he found that his two children had musical talent, he pushed them both into service.

Old Arne managed to ingratiate himself with some theatrical backers, and Susannah was pressed into service at the tender age of seventeen to play the romantic lead in a new musical entertainment called *Amelia* in 1732. It was an unexpected success, and Susannah was particularly singled out for her delicate beauty, solemn manner, and low, emotional voice. She became an audience favorite a year later in her brother's newly formed English Opera Company, playing the title roles in Arne's masque, Rosamond and the Company's pirated production of Handel's *Acis and Galatea*. The latter, as we have seen, was what brought her into Handel's orbit.

The next nine years were harsh ones for the young contralto. The actor-manager of Drury Lane Theatre, Theophilus Cibber, conceived a passion for Susannah, and in the hopes that such a connection would help their theatrical careers, father and son Arne pushed Susannah into marrying him in 1734.

Cibber had been married before, to an actress called Janey Johnson. He was multiply unfaithful to her, worked her shamefully hard, was often drunk, offered her violence, appropriated all the money she earned to pay his gambling debts, and did not bother to attend her funeral when she died of overwork eight years later. That the Arnes wanted this repellent man for Susannah's husband, against her inclination, is testimony to their professional ambitions, most of which came to nothing.

In Susannah, Theophilus found a singing actress of greater skill, refinement, and popularity than his first wife, and he set out to exploit it in every way he could. He promoted her over other, more experienced actresses in the Drury Lane company, and she began to play lead roles at the age of twenty. In an era when theatrical roles were "owned" by actors and actresses, this created significant resentment, felt most keenly by Kitty Clive, the finest comic actress—and biggest money maker—at Drury Lane. But the Polly War was only the worst of the conflicts Theophilus fomented.

The salary Susannah earned for Theophilus did not cover his debts, which continued to mount. Even a smash-and-grab job he perpetrated in a drunken rage on Susannah's costumes and jewelry, which he quickly converted into cash, did not relieve them. Frantic for money, Theophilus hit on a scheme which he believed would solve all his money problems.

He had for some time urged Susannah to allow her many male admirers to pay calls on her, believing they would bestow on her gifts which could go to the cause of his debt relief and to fueling his dissolute lifestyle. She had refused, knowing that the sort of men who generally went in for visits to actresses expected something substantial in return for their attentions. Besides, she was unwell. Two pregnancies had resulted in two infant deaths, and now her husband had given her a venereal disease.

But Theophilus had met a

Theatre Royal, *Drury Lane 1813*, Survey of London, *volume 35*

man of a very different character, William Sloper. He was a young country squire whose father owned an estate in West Woodhay, Berkshire, as well as a large house in London. He admired Susannah to distraction and had already loaned Theophilus £400.

He also had a wife, named Catherine. His father had arranged the marriage, and, while not a love match, it had been fruitful to the extent of two sons. Catherine loved London society (William did not) and came down frequently to the Sloper house in town to see plays and attend fashionable events. In a rare urban excursion, William had accompanied her to see *Othello*, and had seen Susannah play Desdemona. He was smitten. For the rest of the season he contrived to come alone to every single one of Susannah's performances.

When he came calling at the Cibber home, he brought his backgammon board with him and taught Susannah how to play. He was shy and diffident in

Walbury Hill, Combe, Berkshire

company, but when the two were alone, which Theophilus contrived as often as he could, he spoke movingly of the countryside and the bucolic life he treasured. Susannah, searching for quiet and stability, came to value his visits: they meant food in the larder and a husband who kept his temper. William was happy to forgive Theophilus's debt to him and contribute financially to the household. Behind his back, Theophilus called him "Mr. Benefit." In the strongest terms, he encouraged his wife to deepen her relationship with William beyond friendship, and was pleased when this happened. For a time they all lived together, Theophilus ushering Susannah into William's room each night. It was all going exactly to plan. He informed his creditors that they would all soon be paid in full.

What Theophilus did not reckon on was that Susannah and William, both starved for warmth and affection, would fall in love. Susannah asked for a separation from Theophilus, divorce being out of the question, and he refused. So she and William eloped. Suddenly Theophilus saw his cash cow disappear over the horizon, and he hastened to pursue it.

He brought a law suit against William for what in Eighteenth Century England was termed "criminal conversation," that is, alienating the affection of a man or woman from his or her spouse. "A Trial for the Cause of a Criminal Conversation, Theophilus Cibber v. William Sloper, Esquire" was the most sensational court case of its kind of the century. Theophilus's lawyers easily proved the case of adultery. One witness they called was a man whom Theophilus had hired to spy on William and Susannah through eyeholes cut in the wainscoting of their bedroom. In any case, Susannah was pregnant, and the child was certainly William's.

Theophilus asked the court to award him £5000 (over a quarter of a million dollars in today's money). The jury awarded him ten, the smallest amount possible. They deduced correctly that Theophilus had encouraged the relationship and profited from it.

Theopilus extorted more money from William and Susannah for many years thereafter. Susannah was legally bound to return to her husband; her refusal to do so always made William and her vulnerable to Theophilus's financial demands. William having amicably separated from Catherine, he and Susannah retired from public life and went to the country to rear their daughter, Molly.

It was as well they did. The barrister the Sloper family hired to defend William was successful in beating the fine down almost to nothing only by destroying Susannah's reputation. He asserted that William was a naïve young swain, unused to the immoral ways of the town, who had been seduced by a wily and experienced actress. This lie must have hurt and embarrassed Susannah considerably, and we may suppose that William stood for it only because his formidable father insisted on it.

An even more compelling reason for the couple to quit London was that, despite the judge in the case ordering that no official record of it be kept, an unknown person or persons in the courtroom took down the proceedings and turned them into a salacious book, complete with illustrations. It became an immediate sensation and remained in print into Victorian times. Coupled with the court's labelling her a seductress, it spelled disaster for Susannah's career.

The trial took place in 1738. For the next two years, Susannah was content to live obscurely, sometimes even adopting an alias, with William and their child. But in 1741, she decided that she would once more go on stage. Or, at least make the attempt.

Why did she do it? She did not need the money; William was providing more handsomely for her than anyone else had

Lincoln Fields Inn, *Thomas Shephard, 1830*

ever done in her life. The two had not become disenchanted with each other; indeed, they lived together devotedly and respectably for the rest of their lives. Then why subject herself to the trial of trying to regain her place in the theater? The most reasonable conjecture is that, like many an actor before and since, Susannah found that she craved the intoxicating experience of performing. In the beginning, she had not wanted to act; her father had pushed her into it. But once

in, she was well in. Acting completed her personality and empowered her, particularly when she played the pathetic, sympathetic roles which were her forté. Moving audiences to tears and wild applause had proved a powerful drug.

And so she went back. And it took great courage to do so, since she was now considered a living, walking scandal. Many had done what she had done, but they could keep their indiscretions hidden behind closed doors. Susannah's had been trumpeted in court, in every newspaper, and in a best-selling book. Her very name was an appellation of opprobrium and derision. The management at Drury Lane would not hire her; her admirers and friends, she found, had deserted her.

Except one man. James Quin, the leading tragic actor of his day until he was supplanted by Charles Macklin and David

Handel at the Cembalo with his Collaborators

Garrick, had loved playing opposite the meltingly sympathetic Susannah at Drury Lane. To his mind, no one had effectively replaced her; certainly not Kitty Clive, whose Desdemona, which she insisted on playing now that Susannah had vacated the role, was a public byword for bad tragic acting. Too famous and celebrated to care much about public opinion, Quin offered Susannah a season of roles at £300, which she eagerly accepted. And if London would not provide them with a venue for performance, they would desert the ungrateful town.

They would take their act to Dublin. ✤

The Subject is Messiah

Among the most famous letters in the history of music is the one Charles Jennens wrote to his friend, Holdsworth: "Handel says he will do nothing next Winter, but I hope I shall persuade him to set another Scripture Collection I have made for him.... I hope he will lay out his whole Genius and Skill upon it, that the Composition may excell all his former Compositions, as the Subject excells every other Subject. The Subject is Messiah."

Jennens wrote the letter at Gopsal on July 10, 1741, during the period when Handel's gloom at his musical failures was gathering blackest. An article in the April 4th edition of the London Daily Post by "J.B." referred to some outrage that Handel had perpetrated on the public, "a single Disgust...a faux pas made, but not meant." To what can this refer? Did Handel lash out at a public he found undiscerning and ungrateful enough to desert his music? J.B. warned that Handel might be leaving English

shores for good. He called on all men of good sense to forgive whatever fault Handel may have committed and prevent his departure: "If even such a Pride has offended, let us take it as the natural Foible of the great Genius, and let us overlook them like Spots upon the Sun."

Handel spent the summer relatively idle, penning some Italian duets, almost automatically, out of a lifelong habit to write something. He did not leave London as he had contemplated, but then neither did he undertake negotiations with a theater for a new season in the winter. It was almost as if, at this crossroads in his career, he were waiting for something to happen to point out a new direction.

What happened, of course, was Charles Jennens's "scripture collection," and we may here pause briefly in our narrative to consider Jennens's remarkable achievement.

Unlike *Israel in Egypt, Messiah* follows the formal pattern of conventional oratorios, arranged into the traditional arias, recitatives, and choruses. It begins with an instrumental overture, includes a pastoral symphony midway through, and divides neatly into three parts to allow for two intervals, all of which audiences had come to expect.

But the content of *Messiah* was something entirely new. For *Saul*, Jennens had written a compellingly dramatic libretto. For *Messiah*, he followed the practice pioneered in *Israel in Egypt* of creating a libretto entirely from scriptures, in this case

daringly adding New Testament verses. But unlike either of his two previous libretti, *Messiah*, while it contains narrative elements, is not essentially a story. There are no named characters and no single narrator, as in Bach's *Passions*. Instead of a plot, the dramatic through-line of *Messiah* is a theme: the "mystery of Godliness," that is, the whole of Christianity's central doctrines: incarnation, atonement, resurrection, and the eventual universal reign

Upper Part of The Transfiguration, *Raphael, 1520*

of Christ. This Jennens summed up on the title page of the word book by quoting 1 Timothy 3:16 from the New Testament: "And without controversy great is the mystery of godliness: God was manifest in the

Adoration of the Shepherds,
Gerard van Honthorst, 17th C.

flesh, justified in the Spirit, seen of angels, preached unto the Gentiles, believed on in the world, received up into glory." To drive home the point of *Messiah*'s subject matter, he also included a quotation from the apostle Paul's letter to the Colossians: "In whom are hid all the Treasures of Wisdom and Knowledge." That Jennens considered this subject matter greater than that of his previous libretti is indicated by his quotation from Virgil's *Aeneid* on the title page: MAJORA CANAMUS ("Let us sing of greater things.")

This juxtaposition of scriptures on the title page is a portent of Jennens's style in the body of the libretto. It is not only his selection of scriptures which is impressive—and one could argue that the Christian world knows most of these particular scriptures precisely because Jennens chose them for his oratorio—but also the manner in which he arranged them. For example, placing a scripture from Malachi proclaiming that the "Lord...will suddenly come to his Temple" directly after one from Haggai promising that "the Desire of all Nations shall come" creates an immediacy of action brought about entirely by the juxtaposition. This is one of many examples, and it is the hallmark of Jennens's work in the oratorio: weaving together scriptures from all over the Bible into a seamless thematic tapestry.

Commentators on *Messiah* give various titles to the three parts of the oratorio (none was originally given in the libretto). Roughly they are: Part the First (as Jennens styled his divisions)–Prophecies of the coming *Messiah* and the birth; Part the Second–The Passion and its meaning for mankind; Part the Third–Mankind's victory through Christ over death and hell. However, the oratorio also divides in a different manner, by type of scripture, and the two types run through all three parts: narrative verses about the life of Jesus, many of them prophecies drawn from the Old Testament, and doctrinal or admonitory verses.

Seen this way, the oratorio is a skillful dialogue between Christian story and

Sermon on the Mount, *Carl Heinrich Bloch, 19th C.*

Christian belief, and works as a powerful aid to worship for a religion which asks of its adherents faith in both holy events and their meanings. Narrative verses selected by Jennens include, "Behold a Virgin shall conceive..."; "And lo, the Angel of the Lord..."; "And suddenly there was with the Angel..."; "For unto us a Child is born...," "He was despised..."; and "...for the Lord God Omnipotent reigneth..." Verses emphasizing Christian doctrine include: "All we like Sheep..."; "He shall feed his Flock..."; "Come unto Him..."; "O Death, where is thy Sting?"; and "Since by Man came Death..."

The beginning of the oratorio sets the tone, and the juxtaposing style, by employing verses from the fortieth chapter of Isaiah which are first doctrinal—"...comfort ye my People;...speak ye comfortably to Jerusalem...that her Iniquity is pardoned...."; and then narrative—"The Voice of him that crieth in the Wilderness, prepare ye the Way of the Lord..." And

for the end, summing up and bringing to a conclusion both sides of the dialogue, Jennens selects, appropriately, a scripture from the final book of the Bible, Revelations: "Worthy is the Lamb that was slain, and hath redeemed us to God by His Blood, to receive Power, and Riches, and Wisdom, and Strength..."

Taken as a whole, the libretto for *Messi-*

Songs of the Angels, *William-Adolphe Bouguereau, 1881*

ah, once Jennens had penned the last line, had the potential for being the most powerful musical expression of Christian belief ever written. But it was only potential. It would take Handel's music to realize it.

Handel often took an active part in his librettists' work, making suggestions for scenes and musical divisions. There is no evidence that this was the case with *Messiah*. In fact, he may not even have known of its existence until it came his way, probably in July of 1741. Nor, during the period of composition, did Handel consult Jennens. In fact, Jennens seems only to have discovered that his libretto had been set to music after the composition was completed. As he wrote to Holdsworth from his London house in Queen's Square, December 2, 1741: "I heard with great pleasure at my arrival in Town, that Handel had set the Oratorio of *Messiah*..." It is probable that it was this lack of collaboration—or even communication—which caused Jennens's later disgruntlement.

It is delicious to imagine the moment in which Handel opened this strange new manuscript from Jennens and began to read it. What were his thoughts? That he was massively discouraged by his lack of success over the last seasons we know. That he was contemplating leaving London and perhaps even abandoning musical composition we also know. What then caught his eye in Jennens's libretto? There was no story to attract him, after all. What was there which compelled him to take up his pen once more and begin the process which he performed better than any composer of his day, marrying words to music

so perfectly and indissolubly that we cannot imagine them ever again separated?

Of course, Handel, who had read many libretti, and set some weak ones, would have quickly seen the uniqueness and quality of Jennens's text. That alone may have convinced him to set it, for he surely would not have wanted the opportunity to fall to another composer. But was there perhaps something more personal in the scripture collection which attracted him?

Handel's music for the oratorio gives us a clue. Although Jennens had suggested which scriptures should be sung as arias, which as choruses or recitatives, it fell to Handel to make these final decisions. (In fact, he kept on making them over the years, transposing music up and down, turning arias into choruses and back again, depending on the musical forces he had to work with at any given performance of *Messiah*.) And of course it was Handel who determined relative lengths of the individual pieces, whether or not an aria would have a da capo repetition, and so on. And so it is telling that by far the longest of the solo pieces in *Messiah* is the E flat major aria which follows the opening chorus of Part the Second: "He was despised and rejected of Men, a Man of Sorrows, and acquainted with Grief. He gave his Back to the Smiters, and his Cheeks to them that plucked off the Hair; He hid not his Face from Shame and Spitting." Did Handel look at these two verses from different chapters of Isaiah, carefully

Crucifixion, *Diego Valázquez, 17th C.*

stitched together by Jennens to maximize the effect of anguish and meek fortitude, and feel them resonate in his own soul? He, too, had been rejected; he, too, was acquainted with grief; but perhaps, admonished and emboldened by the second scripture, he, too, would not hide his face; yes, he would compose again! And he would draw out these verses into a long da capo aria to show the world the track of his pain.

What adds interest to this conjecture is Handel's having written the aria in Susannah Cibber's contralto register. Although music historians differ on whether or not it was written specifically for her, evidence points in that direction. Handel very deliberately fashioned the aria to be declamatory rather than cantabile, and more than any other piece in the oratorio it depends on sustained emotional expression: the hallmark of Susannah's singing style. Did he hope with it to coax his favorite English female singer out of re-

tirement? She, too, he must have known, knew something of being despised and rejected and acquainted with grief. That

Handel

the aria is the longest in *Messiah* allows us to dwell on the sufferings of its title character. Was Handel's lengthy musical realization of it also one soul in distress crying out to another? Perhaps this is at the heart of why he chose to set Jennens's remarkable libretto.

Handel began to compose *Messiah* on August 22, a Saturday, completing the

Handel's House, *John Buckler, watercolour, 1839.*
© Handel House Collections Trust.

drafting of Part the First on the next Friday, August 28; Part the Second, the following Sunday, September 6; and Part the Third six days later on Saturday, September 12. He followed his practiced procedure in composing, writing all the single leading vocal or instrumental lines—the tunes—first, for the entire oratorio, inserting the recitative texts where needed (for *Messiah* there were few of these). This was the hard work, the heavy lifting: inventing or adapting tunes. The majority of the music in *Messiah* is original to the piece, and many, including Handel, would later borrow from this amazing treasure trove of tunes. The melodies for five pieces in the oratorio, however, are adaptations of his Italian duets, including two which he had penned just weeks before. They became the choruses, "His Yoke is easy..." and

"For unto us a Child is born."

He found little to alter in Jennens's text. It was, after all, published scripture from the Authorized Version of the Bible, and Handel could not therefore simply change, shorten, or lengthen a passage to better fit his musical conception, as he habitually did with other libretti. However, when he found Jennens's choice of a scripture about feet (Isaiah 52:7–9) cumbersome and overly long, he substituted a shorter, more sprightly verse on the same subject (Romans 10:15).

The entire oratorio supplied with a melodic through-line, Handel then accomplished what he called "filling up"—adding in all the harmonies and orchestrations—in an astonishing two days. He was finished by September 14th, having completed his musical odyssey in twenty-four days. After about a week of rest, his confidence as a composer renewed, he plunged into the composition of his next oratorio, *Samson*.

The room where Messiah *was composed in Handel House.*
© Matthew Hollow

Anecdotes abound about Handel's behavior during the period of *Messiah*'s composition, all recorded well after the fact. As one sifts through them, it is not possible to ascertain for certain which have the greatest claim on truth. Given his epicurean nature—and the fact that he employed a cook—the story that he refused food and drink while penning *Messiah* is difficult to credit. The sheer physical labor of committing notes to 260 manuscript pages would have required considerable fuel; and for Handel, that fuel would have been gourmet. For some there may be a connection between inspiration and asceticism; not for Handel.

He was sincerely religious, if not devoted to any one denomination. A Lutheran by birth, Handel composed music for Catholic, Anglican, and Calvinist services as well as for those of his own faith. During his many years in London, he regularly attended St. George's Hanover Square, an Anglican church a few minutes walk from his home on Brook Street. His religious nature, then, was ecumenical within a Christian framework, a condition which may have contributed to his being attracted to Jennens's nondenominational manuscript. It is not therefore at all out of the question that he really said what has been attributed to him and repeated for more than two centuries about an experience he had while composing *Messiah*: "I did think I did see all Heaven before me and the great God

Handel. *Thomas Hudson*

Himself." Neither before nor after the composition of *Messiah* did Handel ever claim to be a visionary man, but its sacred source material and his intense concentration during its composition—and, may it be said?—a divine foreknowledge on the part of the Giver of Visions that *Messiah* would offer much hope to a weary world, may have called forth that sublime experience. Equally plausible, and on the same grounds, is the statement attributed to him about the composition of the Hallelujah Chorus specifically: "Whether I was in my body or out of my body as I wrote it I know not. God knows." And certainly the anecdote related by Burney in a letter penned in 1776 has the ring of authenticity. He wrote that an English lady of refinement, after having attended a rehearsal for *Messiah* and being greatly moved, asked Handel what had made it possible for him, a foreigner "who understood the English Language but imperfectly, to enter so fully into the sublime spirit of the Words." According to Burney, Handel replied, "Madam, I thank God I have a little religion." The understated, dry wit is surely Handelian.

In the spring or summer, Handel had received an invitation from the Lord Lieutenant of Ireland, the 3rd Duke of Devonshire, to perform a season of his music in Dublin. He had meant not to perform again anywhere. But then he had also meant not to compose again—until he had read Charles Jennens's manuscript.

He had arranged nothing with theater owners in London and, probably, the prospect of facing the town after his "single disgust" and the failure of the previous season did not appeal. For thirty years he had spent the autumn and winter performing in London; perhaps it was time for a change of scenery. Yes, he would go to Ireland! *Messiah* was already doing its work of giving hope, first to the only man who had already heard it, its composer. Handel packed up some of his recent compositions together with his newly minted oratorio, persuaded the soprano Christina Avolio to come sing with him—and boarded the packet from Parkgate.

Thus, when Jennens arrived in London, he found Handel gone. He was pleased to discover that the composer had set his scripture collection, as noted earlier, "but it was some mortification to me," he wrote to Holdsworth, "to hear that instead of performing it here he was gone into Ireland with it. However, I hope we shall hear it when he comes back."

Handel arrived in Dublin on November 18, an event of sufficient importance to be announced in the *Dublin Journal*.

Susannah Cibber, he learned, would arrive shortly. ❦

Handel's plan was to offer one or two series of concerts, to which patrons

That Generous and Polite Nation

In Dublin, Handel took up lodging in a house on Abbey Street and straightaway entered into the town's music scene. On December 10, the service at St. Andrew's Church featured his music, along with a sermon from Dr. Patrick Delaney, Chancellor of St. Patrick's Cathedral. Handel quickly engaged Matthew Dubourg to act as his concert-master, happy to find him once more available and disposed to be so engaged. And he visited both cathedrals in town, St. Patrick's and Christ Church, to form a choir for his performances and to audition choristers for solo parts.

could buy subscriptions. Each subscription would include three tickets for each performance, as well as passes to attend final rehearsals. The concerts would take place not in a theater, but at a new purpose-built concert building on Fishamble Street. Called the Music Hall, and opened just two months before, it was a

St. Patrick Cathedral, Dublin

large room with good acoustics designed to seat six hundred. The first subscription series was to feature the oratorio *Esther*; the masques, *L'Allegro Il Penseroso ed Il Moderato* and *Acis and Galatea*; and various concerti. Subscriptions sold out very quickly, the Duke of Devonshire's name leading the list of subscribers.

Susannah Cibber docked at Dublin port about a week after Handel's arrival to join Quin, who had played through the summer at the Theatre Royal on Aungier Street with none other than Kitty Clive, who deliberately left Dublin before Susannah arrived. She and Quin had done very well financially playing knock-about farce and comedy, though there was no love lost between them. But Quin now looked forward with great anticipation to playing more high-minded works with Susannah.

There is no record of William or Molly accompanying Susannah to Dublin (the *Journal* announced her arrival as a solo event), and it may be that she spent her time in Dublin without them.

Howth Harbour, Dublin

On the other hand, William had become wary of publicity by this time, and he and Molly could easily have slipped over from Parkgate on another of the packet ships which made the crossing four times each week. Either by herself or with her lover and child, Susannah took up residence in a house Quin had prepared for her on Aungier Street and settled down to intensive rehearsals.

Quin's plan was for her to play some fifteen roles, many of them new to her, ranging from Isabella and Desdemona in Shakespeare's *Measure for Measure* and *Othello* to the female leads in *Love's Last Shift* by her father-in-law, Colley Cibber, and *The Fair Penitent* by Nicholas Rowe. It would be de-

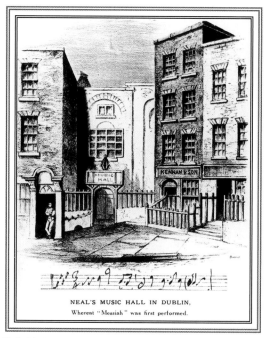

NEAL'S MUSIC HALL IN DUBLIN,
Whereat "Messiah" was first performed.

Neal's Music Hall, Dublin, where his oratorio 'Messiah' was first performed,
19th century engraving by unnamed artist

manding, but, after years of being away from the stage, we can imagine how eagerly Susannah plunged into learning her parts. Finally, she would once again tread the boards! First up was one of her sure-fire roles, Indiana in *The Conscious Lovers*, which she was to play opposite Quin's Bevil. Susannah's long-anticipated debut came on December 12, two days after Handel's church music was played at St. Andrew's.

It was not auspicious. The Dublin public, though no doubt eager to see the celebrated London actress who had chosen their city to re-launch her career, were not certain if it was within the bounds of decorum and decency to patronize a woman who was ashamed to show her face in her own country. The house was practically empty. Management took in only £10, and it would not have escaped Susannah's notice that this was the same amount awarded her husband at her adultery trial. The theatrical season, planned by Quin and Susannah with such optimism and promise, looked to be stillborn.

Handel may have been at this dismal debut. He had every reason to attend. He was looking for female soloists; he would have read the notices of Susannah's coming-out performance; and in the back of his mind, if not further forward, was the knowledge that he had written an aria close to his heart for Susannah's register.

However, Handel had his own season of performances to put in place, and this had to take priority. Notices were very good after the first concert of his subscription series, given at the Music Hall on December 23. The *Dublin Journal* enthused, "The Performance was superior to any Thing of the Kind in this Kingdom before; and our Nobility and Gentry to show their Taste for all Kinds of

Theatre Royal, Drury Lane, 1674

*Letter from Handel to Charles Jennens at Gopsall,
dated 16 July 1744.
In this letter, Handel's writes to Charles Jennens
about his texts for* Belshazzar *and* Messiah.
© Handel House Collections Trust

ed in Dublin. By this we understand that Jennens believed the oratorio would be performed there, though its title was not announced in Handel's initial subscription series. Handel's lengthy response to Jennens, dated December 29, gives a strong indication of how happy he was with his reception in Dublin: "The Nobility did me the Honour to make amongst themselves a Subscription for 6 Nights, which did fill a Room of 600 Persons...and without Vanity the Performance was received

Handel at home

Genius, expressed their great Satisfaction, and have already given all imaginable Encouragement to this grand Musick." The other concerts in the series were equally successful, the Duke of Devonshire, and often his family, attending all six.

At about this time, Jennens sent over from London the quotations he wished Handel to include on the title page of *Messiah* when he had the word book print-with a general Approbation...the Musick sounds delightfully in this charming Room, which puts me in such Spirits (and my Health being so good) that I exert my self on my Organ with more than usual Success.... I cannot sufficiently express the kind treatment I receive here, but the Politeness of this generous Nation cannot be unknown to You, so I let you judge of the Satisfaction I enjoy, passing my time with Honour, profit, and pleasure." In high good humor, Handel quickly announced a second concert series of a further six performances, at "the Desire of several Persons of Quality and Distinction," as the *Journal* announced. The program for the second series included the masque, Alexander's Feast and a concert version of his Italian opera *Imeneo*.

But to perform these well Handel would need his contralto.

In his official capacity as Lord Lieutenant of Ireland The Duke of Devonshire never again experienced so personally

demanding a cultural season as that of 1741–42. Not only did he support all of Handel's concert performances with his personal attendance, but he was also called upon by the management of the Aungier Street Theatre, panicked by their suddenly drafty house, to put his imprimatur on the theatrical season being offered by Quin and Susannah. He readily agreed to

Lord Lieutenant of Ireland, William Cavendish, 3rd Duke of Devonshire

lend his official support. And so, the day after Susannah's disastrous debut in *The Conscious Lovers*, an announcement was printed in Faulkner's *Dublin Journal* that "By their Graces', the Duke and Duchess of Devonshire's special Command, on Thursday next at the Theatre Royal in Aungier Street will be acted Venice Preserved...Pierre by Mr. Quin, Belvidera by Mrs. Cibber, being the second time of her Performance in the Kingdom." The announcement of the Lord Lieutenant's official approval of Susannah was the magic charm. The public threw off its squeamishness and came to Aungier Street Theatre in droves. From then on, Susannah and Quin played to capacity houses.

And now Susannah had more parts to rehearse than those of dramatic heroines.

After Handel engaged Susannah to sing in his second subscription series, it must have seemed like old times for composer and singer, rehearsing at Handel's Abbey Street lodging. No doubt, he was just as painstaking with her as formerly, going over each musical phrase until Susannah learned it by ear. There were parts to learn in all three musical pieces *Esther*, Alexander's Feast, and *Imeneo*. And then, though it was not on the program for the second series, there would have been a moment when he shared with her his new oratorio and the aria he had written with her in mind. What thoughts went through Susannah's head as she read the text—"He was despised and rejected of Men, a Man of Sorrows, and acquainted with Grief,"—and noted its length? It went on and on, just as, she must have felt, her ordeal had. Here at last was the piece of music which would allow her to give vent to all her shame and grief, written perfectly for her particular talents.

With Handel and Susannah now joining forces with Dubourg and Signora Avolio and a choir and other soloists selected from St. Patrick's and Christ Church, the second subscription season, given in March and early April, 1742, was an even greater sensation. Patrons were requested to leave their carriages or sedan chairs down the street to avoid clogging the entrance to the Music Hall.

A spoke in the wheel had occurred a little earlier when the dean of St. Patrick's Cathedral, Dr. Jonathan Swift (of Gulliver's Travels fame) suddenly revoked his permission to lend his cathedral's choristers "to a club of fiddlers in Fishamble

Street," but this was soon cleared up. Sadly, Swift was verging on insanity at this time, and the sub-dean quietly arranged for the choristers to continue.

Reverand Johnathan Swift

Before the second subscription series came to its successful conclusion, a notice appeared in the Dublin Journal, on March 27, announcing an additional concert to be given during Holy Week: "For Relief of the Prisoners in the several Gaols, and for the Support of Mercer's Hospital in Stephen's Street and of the Charitable Infirmary on the Inns Quay, on Monday the 12th of April [later corrected to Tuesday the 13th], will be performed at the Musick Hall in Fishamble Street, Mr. Handel's new Grand Oratorio, call'd the *MESSIAH*, in which the Gentlemen of the Choirs of both Ca-

thedrals will assist, with some Concertoes on the Organ, by Mr. Handell." Tickets cost half a guinea each and, as in the two series, included a free pass to the rehearsal held on Friday, April 9.

A word needs to be said here about Handel's performances for charities. Though too epicurean and cantankerous, particularly with members of his own profession, to ever be considered a saint, he was, rain or shine, in good times and bad for his personal economy, a practitioner of the Christian virtue of charity. He was a founding—and always paid up—member of the Fund for the Support of Decay'd Musicians, the function of which was to raise and maintain a perpetual fund to support retired musicians and their families. Handel also frequently gave benefit concerts and other performances for charities or for the personal enrichment of performers in his companies. It is worthy of note that not only the Dublin premiere, but many other subsequent performances of *Messiah* under Handel's direction benefited one charity or other, tangible instances of the oratorio doing its work of spreading hope in the world.

The Friday rehearsal of *Messiah* was well

The Opera House, *Haymarket, by Augustus Pugin and Thomas Rowlandson for Ackermann's* Microcosm of London *(1808-1811)*

attended. The next day's *Journal* reported those who went as "a most Grand, Polite, and crouded Audience" and called the oratorio "the finest Composition of Mu-

sick that ever was heard, and the sacred Words as properly adapted for the Occasion." The article went on to make a most unusual request. Anticipating an overcapacity crowd in the Music Hall for the premiere performance the following week, it requested "as a Favour, that the Ladies who honour this Performance with their Presence would be pleased to come without Hoops [hoop-framed skirts], as it will greatly increase the Charity, by making Room for more company." On the day of the performance, the newspaper printed an article requesting the "Gentlemen" attending "to come without their Swords" for the same reason.

The first performance of Handel's *Messiah* took place in the Music Hall on Fishamble Street, Dublin, at noon on Tuesday, April 13, 1742. It was Holy Week, Easter falling on April 18 that year. The choir for that first performance was made up of about sixteen men and as many boys. Soloists included, besides Susannah and Christina Avolio as contralto and soprano, men from the choirs: John Hill and John Mason, basses; James Bailey, tenor; and sharing contralto duties with Susannah, Cathedral altos, William Lamb and Joseph Ward. No instrumentalists are named, apart from concert-master Dubourg, but the orchestra was made up of a string band reinforced occasionally by oboes and bassoons, trumpets and timpani. Handel, of course, led them all from his seat at the harpsichord.

Susanna Cibber, *John Faber after Thomas Hudson, mezzotint engraving, 1746.*
© *Handel House Collections Trust.*

In attendance that day was Patrick Delaney, the man who had preached at the service featuring Handel's music the previous December. He was recently bereaved of his wife, and his feelings were still tender. He had almost certainly never heard Susannah Cibber sing—he was only attending this Holy Week performance as an act of piety—and so he was unaware of the effect Susannah could have on listeners. As the Irish actor Thomas Sheridan, also in attendance that day, noted, "by a natural pathos and perfect conception of the words, she often penetrated the heart, when others with infinitely greater skill could only reach the ear." Perhaps Dr. Delaney, therefore, was caught off guard when Susannah rose midway through the oratorio to sing her aria, "He was despised..." When the last strains of it died away—"He hid not his Face from Shame and Spitting"—and before the choir could launch into the solemn chorus, "Surely he hath borne our Griefs...", Dr. Delaney rose and with tears in his eyes proclaimed fervently in a voice heard throughout the Hall, "Woman, for this, be all thy sins forgiven."

It was enough. Susannah must have felt herself reborn that day. Despite the tribulations to come, on that April afternoon, she felt herself accepted and acceptable.

The sum collected for distribution to the named charities at *Messiah*'s initial performance was £400. The acclaim for the oratorio was instant and vociferous. The *Dublin Journal* opined: "Words are wanting to express the exquisite Delight it afforded to the admiring crouded Audience. The Sublime, the Grand, and the Tender, adapted to the most elevated, majestick and moving Words, conspired to trans-

port and charm the ravished Heart and Ear." Dr. Edward Synge, Bishop of Elphin, noted in a letter that Handel "seems to have excell'd himself. The whole is beyond any thing I had a notion of till I Read and heard it. It Seems to be a Species of Musick different from any other." He was particularly impressed that "tho the young & gay of both Sexes were present in great numbers, their behaviour was uniformly grave & decent, which Show'd that they were not only pleas'd but affect'd with the performance."

Messiah was performed a second time,

David Garrick, *Thomas Gainsborough*

along with some organ concerti played by Handel, at the composer's final concert in Dublin on June 3rd. On that occasion, it was announced in the Journal, "a Pane of Glass will be removed from the Top of each of the Windows" to help cool the Hall.

On August 13, Handel departed the city that had done so much to revive his career and renew his spirit. He clearly meant to return the next winter for another season of performances, as he wrote in a letter to Jennens, but in the event, he never visited Ireland again. Susannah left ten days later on the 23rd, taking ship with a young Irish actor who would revolutionize the English theater, David Garrick. By September, Handel was back in London. He wrote to Jennens on the 9th: "As for my Success in General in that generous and polite Nation, I reserve the full account of it till I have the Honour to see you in London."

That honor would come soon. And trouble was brewing. ❦

A view of Whitehall looking south, 1740

Notwithstanding the Clamor Rais'd Against It

Handel's first tasks upon returning to London were to arrange with Rich for performances at Covent Garden Theatre and to secure singers and instrumentalists for them. He had brought Dubourg with him from Dublin to act as concert-master, and he had retained both Christina Avolio and Susannah Cibber as singers. To these he added Beard, Savage, Reinhold, Lowe, and the soprano Miss Edwards. He also hired, chiefly to play Delilah in his new oratorio *Samson*, Kitty Clive, who seemed completely right for the role. But she would also sing in *Messiah*.

What she and Susannah thought about sharing a stage once again we can only conjecture. The Polly War was six years behind them by now; still, it is hard to imagine there was not some residual resentment, and Kitty had avoided Susannah in Dublin. But they were both professionals, used to working with those with whom they did not have a congenial personal relationship, particularly the fiery and combative Kitty. In any event, they would not be acting together. Handel was done with moving actors about on stage in musical dramas. *Samson* would be a concert performance, as *Imeneo* had been in Dublin, and any char-acterization not inherently in the text and score would have to be attempted without costume and standing in one place, facing the audience.

He announced in the London news-papers for February 12th a subscription series of six concerts beginning the following Monday, February 18th. He had other rehearsed pieces of music at the ready, in case *Samson*, like his previous oratorios and operas in the 1741–42 season, failed to please and had to be pulled from the stage quickly. He must have held his breath as the night of the 18th approached. Everything he performed, including his new work *Messiah*, had been a roaring success in Dublin; could he ever again achieve success on stage with a new work in London?

He could. London responded rapturously to *Samson*, Handel breathed again, and he played nothing else for his subscription of six concerts. Rich must have felt he was on to a good thing, with a refreshed and buoyant Handel filling his theater. A second subscription season was immediately announced, to begin March 16. It would commence with a reprise of *Samson*, follow with L'Allegro, and then, it was announced, a second new oratorio would premiere. It was called, mysteriously, *A New Sacred Oratorio*.

Why did Handel change the name of *Messiah* in his announcements? To learn the answer to that question, we must examine more of the correspondence of Handel's talented, prickly librettist, Charles Jennens.

Jennens had responded to Handel's let-

Handel

ter including the laudatory remarks from Bishop Elphin about *Messiah* with one of his own to Holdsworth, dated October 29: "...I hope to have some very agreeable Entertainments from him this Season. His *Messiah* by all accounts is his Masterpiece." His pleasurable anticipation of seeing *Messiah* in London turned to displeasure, however, when he received the word book of the oratorio and, presumably, the score. Of the libretto, he wrote to Holdsworth the next February, "I have a copy, as it was printed in Ireland, full of Bulls [printing errors]; & if he does not print a correct one here, I shall do it my Self & perhaps tell him a piece of my mind by way of Preface. I am a little out of humour, as you perceive..."

What put Jennens out of humor was more than the discovery of printing errors in his libretto. Jennens was a competent amateur musician, and a partial piano reduction of *Messiah*'s score exists in his hand. Apparently he had scrutinized the score closely and had found it wanting. "His *Messiah* has disappointed me," he wrote to Holdsworth in January, "being set in great hast[e], tho' he said he would be a year about it & make it the best of all his Compositions. I shall put no more Sacred Words into his hands, to be thus abus'd." He pe-

titioned Handel with increasing forcefulness all through the late winter and spring of 1743 to make improvements to the score, but to no avail: "As to *Messiah*," he wrote Holdsworth, "'tis still in his power by retouching the weak parts to make it fit for a publick performance; & I have said

The Way of the World Performance, 1732, Covenant Garden Theatre

a great deal to him on the Subject; but he is so lazy & so obstinate, that I much doubt the Effect." Jennens's silly, specious accusation of sloth reveals much about the temper into which the librettist had whipped himself, nothing at all about Handel's work habits. Going to see *Samson* at Covent Garden made him angrier still: "Last Friday Handel perform'd his *Samson*, a most exquisite Entertainment, which tho' I heard with infinite Pleasure, yet it increas'd my resentment for his neglect of *Messiah*." Even an enlightened heathen, he wrote, would not prefer the story of *Samson* "to the sublime Sentiments & expressions of Isaiah & David, of the Apostles & Evangelists, & of Jesus

Christ." And yet, to Jennens's mind, Handel had obviously lavished his attentions on the Hebrew strong man and left his Lord and Savior to languish. He passed this judgment on before he—or anyone else in England—had yet heard a note of *Messiah* performed.

Among those who had never heard even a portion of this music was a set of people who now stood out to oppose its performance. In Dublin, no clergy except the unbalanced Dr. Swift had thought to utter a word of criticism against the oratorio. In fact, as we have seen, some men of the cloth—Dr. Delaney, the Bishop of Elphin—were greatly moved by it precisely because of its potent combination of sublime music and holy words. But in London, where the clergy had been eyeing oratorios with increasing alarm for many years, the opposite opinion held sway among some of the more influential. A warning shot had been fired across Handel's bow in 1732 when the Bishop

of London had prevented boy choristers of the Chapel Royal from singing in a fully staged production of *Esther* at the Haymarket Theatre. He and others of his mind objected to oratorio on two grounds: first, its subject matter was sacred and therefore not suitable for turning into entertainment with secular (read: opera) music; and second, that placing words from the Bible in a theater and allowing them to be sung by lay persons, no matter how talented, smacked of blasphemy—particularly given the reputations of some of the singers. This walling off of the sacred from the secular lay at the heart of the objection to oratorio.

And now those objections rose to a fever pitch. "What adds to my chagrin," Jennens wrote to Holdsworth, "is, that if [Handel] makes his Oratorio ever so perfect, there is a clamour about Town, said to arise from the Bishops, against performing it." Well, of course—if turning the stories of mortals—*Esther, Saul, Samson*—into entertainment verged on sacrilege, how much more blasphemous to subject Divinity to the same treatment. And then to drag the Incarnation and the Passion into the public theater, where the lewd regularly roared at the antics of the latest coarse comedy—it was tantamount to serving the Host as a meal in a tavern.

Most horrifying of all to some of the bishops' way of thinking was the woman Cibber, whom Handel had hired to swell the ranks of his singers. Had the man no shame? Would she be mouthing Holy Writ? Was it appropriate that this infamous adulteress—and it was well known that she had not repented of her wickedness and returned to her husband—profanely warble the sufferings of Jesus? It was intolerable. It was equivalent to the Whore of Babylon cynically reciting the Lord's Prayer.

What could Handel do? As he heard the rumblings of some in the clergy—many, of course, found no objection to his oratorios—he could or would not cancel his performance of *Messiah*. Nor could he produce it in a location other than the theater he had engaged. (Certainly no church would accept it.) Nor would he discharge any of his singers, least of all Susannah, whose emotional delivery was the heart of the performance. What he could do, he would. If the word, "*Messiah*", on a playbill or in an advertisement

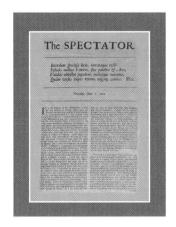

gave offense, he would change that. He would call it *A New Sacred Oratorio* and hope for the best. Rehearsals continued apace.

And then on Saturday, March 19, just five days before *Messiah* was set to premiere, the storm broke in the press. The Universal Spectator published a lengthy letter by an anonymous party calling himself Philalethes (lover of truth). Philalethes, whoever he was, spoke for all in the town who objected to oratorios and to *Messiah* particularly. And his clear intent was to enlist others to his cause. "My...Purpose... is to consider, and, if possible, induce others to consider, the Impropriety of Oratorios, as they are now perform'd," he wrote. "An Oratorio either is an Act of Religion, or it is not; if it is, I ask if the Playhouse is a fit Temple to perform it in, or a Company of Players fit Ministers of God's Word...? If it is...perform'd...but for Diversion and Amusement...what a Profanation of God's Name and Word is this, to make so light Use of them?... But it seems the Old Testament is not to be prophan'd alone...but the New must be join'd with it, and God by the most sacred the most merciful name of *Messiah*. ...I must again ask, If the Place and Performers are fit?"

All who read the letter would have known that Philalethes's double emphasis on the fitness of the singers was meant to call publicly into question the fitness, particularly, of Susannah Cibber. It had taken the Lord Lieutenant of Ireland's presence at Aungier Street Theatre to square her with

George III statue, soho, John Nest

the Dublin public. In London, only one man could work the same magic. Susannah—and Handel, no doubt—waited in vain through the rest of the week and weekend for a notice in a newspaper saying that the Royal Presence would grace the London premiere of *Messiah*. But the King had not come for years. They knew he would not come now.

Philalethes did not go unanswered. "A Gentleman, on reading the Universal Spectator," responded in verse a few days later. He put the case for those who supported oratorio performance: "Cease, Zealots, cease to blame these heav'nly Lays, For Seraphs fit to sing *Messiah*'s Praise! Nor, for your trivial Argument, assign, 'The Theatre not fit for Praise Divine.' These hallow'd Lays to Musick give new Grace, To Virtue Awe, and sanctify the Place; To Harmony, like his, Celestial Pow'r is giv'n, T'exalt the Soul from Earth, and make, of Hell, a Heav'n."

The oratorio would have its supporters at the premiere, even if its detractors convinced many to stay away.

The King would have been advised by his bishops to be among those missing, given the controversy swirling around *Messiah*. It would not do to affix the royal imprimatur by attending: one of the King's titles was, after all, *Fidei Defen-*

Drury Lane Theatre, 1808

sor, Defender of the Faith. And yet the subject matter would have appealed to George II, still bereft, still mourning the death of a wife to whom he had been so attached: "The trumpet shall sound, and the dead shall awake!" Yes, it would have been tempting.

Finally the sun rose on Wednesday, March 23rd, the day of the first performance. It is difficult not to wonder about the mental and emotional states of those connected with *Messiah*.

For most of the singers and instrumentalists, it mattered little whether the house was large or small; they would be paid, whatever the size. Still, knowing about the controversy surrounding the new piece, they surely hoped to get through the performance without untoward incident in the audience.

Matthew Dubourg had seen reactions

Handel, *Balthasar Denner*

to Handel's music ranging from the rapturous to the sullen. It was the composer's music, itself, that attracted him and kept him playing with Handel. And he knew, from having played it twice in Dublin, that even by Handelian standards *Messiah* was something extraordinary.

Tenor John Beard was feeling unwell. But he would certainly not let his old friend down by scratching when he was needed most; he would husband his strength through the day and hope to have sufficient energy to perform at his peak that evening. (In the event, he had to excuse himself after the first performance. Handel quickly reassigned his parts among the other soloists for the second night.)

Kitty Clive was finally getting the chance she had always wanted to make the jump from acting comic parts to being taken seriously in a serious role. This was especially important because younger actresses at Drury Lane, especially the versatile Peg Woffington, were nipping at her heels. She had done well as Delilah in *Samson*, but tonight she would sing verses from the Bible. It was an important night for her.

Charles Jennens was perhaps in a quandary as to whether or not even to attend the performance, so disappointed was he by Handel's music, which he found insufficiently grand, composed for too few instruments, and possessed of too many borrowings (one would have been too many for Jennens). Still, it was his scripture collection being performed. In the end, dressed like a lord and attended by footmen, he went.

For Susannah, who must have known that she was the person whose "fitness" to sing scripture was most being challenged in the Philalethes letter, it would have taken extraordinary courage to face

the London public again. The last it had seen of her was as a disgraced and ridiculed object of scorn. Many in the audience would have seen the illustrated book written from the adultery trial; some, no doubt, owned a copy. And yet, she knew that if she was to return to the life which truly fulfilled her, it would have to be in London. Generous Dublin was too far away from William and his estates. And there was Molly to think of now.

King George II, After a portrait from studio of T Hudson, NPG, Player's Cigarettes, Kings & Queens of England, 38 of 50

George Frederick Handel stood at a crossroads on the night of *Messiah*'s London premiere. His Italian opera days were irrevocably behind him. Ahead of him, stretching out in a vista his artistic mind's eye could see to the far horizon, was idea after idea for new oratorios. *Samson* had succeeded. If *Messiah* was also successful, he must have felt, it would be substantial evidence that the town was ready to follow him into this new musical adventure.

And so the evening came, and the performance began. The house was not large; Philalethes and his ilk had seen to that. As the Earl of Shaftsbury later recalled, "...partly from the Scruples some Persons had entertained against carrying on such a Performance in a Play House, and partly for not entering into the genius of the Composition, this Capital Composition was but indifferently relish's."

But the King was in the Royal Box; in the end, he could not stay away, despite the worried cluckings of the bishops. Handel's music had always thrilled and uplifted him. Did he not deserve to exercise the royal prerogative and hear the glad message of resurrection and eternal life in a way that would stir him and make him believe once more?

To Handel onstage, it was enough that His Majesty was in the audience. Whatever the size of the house tonight, where the King trod others would eventually follow. It was like old times seeing him in the Royal Box, even though he looked lonely without his Caroline.

From the harpsichord, Handel gives the downbeat and the brief overture plays. And then Beard steps forward to sing the first recitative: "Comfort ye, comfort ye, my People, saith your God."

The audience can hardly breathe. It is as though Scripture is coming to life.

Aria follows aria—tenor, soprano, contralto, bass—punctuated by choruses and connected by recitatives. Beard finds his strength; Kitty sings, and no one laughs. After the second interval Susannah steps forward: "He was despised, rejected." This time there is no Patrick Delaney in the audience to intone his approval, but there is another who has lost a wife sitting in the Royal Box, and perhaps he, too, is moved by Susannah's heartfelt singing.

There is no plot, and yet a story is being told: A man who is also God comes to earth as a frail human who suffers and is slain. And by his death violence and sorrow and sin, and even death, itself, pass away, and mankind is redeemed and reconciled. "O Death, where is thy Sting? O grave, where is thy Victory?" And this resurrected Man of Sorrows lives still, the oratorio is saying, and will come again in glory to the earth to rule and reign. "Hallelujah!"

As the choir sings this chorus, the audience looks up to the Royal Box to find the King on his feet. Has the Fidei Defensor risen in indignation, perhaps to stop the oratorio at last, finally convinced that the bishops are right and *Messiah* is a blasphemy? No. As James Beattie wrote of the moment years later to the Reverend Dr. Laing, "When Handel's *Messiah* was first performed, the audience was exceedingly struck and affected by the music in general, but when that chorus struck up, 'For the Lord God Omnipotent reigneth', they were so transported that they all, together with the king (who happened to be present), started up, and remained standing till the chorus ended: and hence it became the fashion in England for the audience to stand while that part of the music is performing." His Majesty is standing to acknowledge the coming reign of a King mightier than he, one who, he fervently hopes, will one day bring about a reunion with his Caroline. All in the audience stand with him. Tonight, for a few moments, the theater has been transformed into a temple, "fit for Praise Divine."

When the final "Amen" sounds, and the oratorio concludes, it has wrought perhaps its greatest miracle of the night: it has managed to please Charles Jennens—almost. He wrote to Holdsworth the next day: "*Messiah* was perform'd last night, & it will be again to morrow, notwithstanding the clamour rais'd against it, which has only occasion'd it's being advertis'd without its Name; a Farce, which gives me as much offence as any thing relating to the performance can give the Bishops & other squeamish People. 'Tis after all, in the main, a fine Composition, notwithstanding some weak parts..." ❧

Their Sound Is Gone Out into All Lands

Messiah played twice more, along with another performance of *Samson*, and Handel's 1743 season as Covent Garden came to a successful conclusion on March 31st. Perhaps a desire to avoid controversy kept Handel from reviving Messiah the following year, but in 1745 he performed the oratorio with some of the changes Jennens had been nagging him to make—converting what had been a tenor aria, "Their Sound is gone out...", into a chorus, for example—to conclude that year's season at Covent Garden. This set the pattern. From then until the close of Handel's life, Covent Garden Theatre became his permanent home, and he invariably ended seasons there with Messiah, usually performed shortly before Easter. The last of his music he heard in his mortal life was a performance of Messiah given at Covent Garden on April 6, 1759. He died eight days later.

John Beard recovered his health fully and continued as one of Handel's most stalwart performers, singing, among other parts, the tenor role in *Messiah* on many occasions. He became a share-holder in Covent Garden Theatre, when John Rich, who was his father-in-law, died in 1761. Matthew Dubourg returned to Dublin, resuming his role as Master and Composer of State Music until 1752.

He continued indulging his passion for adapting Irish folk tunes into orchestral arrangements, penning Variations of Druid Tunes and several sonatas. He also continued playing with Handel and was named a beneficiary in the composer's will. Kitty Clive, always one to land on her feet, thrived under the new management of David Garrick at Drury Lane Theatre, playing twenty-two more years in his company and eventually retiring to a leafy suburb of southwest London into a villa which came to be called "Cliveden," given her by Horace Walpole." Throughout her long career, she continued to sing occasionally with Handel, who became a valued friend.

Susannah Cibber's career in London was entirely resuscitated by her roles in Samson and *Messiah* in Handel's 1743 season. She continued to sing in *Messiah* and in other of Handel's concerts for charity throughout her life. Living happily with William Sloper, she saw their daughter, Molly, successfully married to a respectable, kind husband. When Susannah also joined Garrick's company at Drury Lane, she largely avoided conflicts with Kitty by specializing in dramatic and, especially, tragic roles, eventually building a reputation as one of the finest actresses of her era. When Garrick heard of her death in 1766, he is said to have remarked, "Then tragedy dies with her."

She was given burial at Westminster Abbey, one of the very few actors ever so honored. And what would Philalethes have thought of that?

Messiah opened the floodgates to Handel's creative genius as a composer of oratorios and masques, and the years following its premiere saw him produce an extraordinary body of work: Semele and Joseph and His Brethren (1743), Hercules and Belshazzar (1744, the latter with a libretto by Jennens), The Occasional Oratorio and Judas Maccabaeus (1746), Joshua and Alexander Balus (1747), Susanna and Solomon (1748), *Theodora* (1749), The Choice of Hercules (1750), and Jephtha (1751). Together with Saul, *Israel in Egypt*, and L'Allegro, they are the pinnacle of the English oratorio, *Messiah* taking pride of place at the very top.

May 1st, 1750, marked an important new direction for *Messiah* performances. The year before, Handel had begun his association with the Hospital for the

Knights of the Bath, *Canaletto, 1749*

Maintenance and Education of Exposed and Deserted Young Children, or Foundling Hospital, giving a noon-time charity concert which included a new pastiche, the Foundling Hospital Anthem with the "Hallelujah Chorus" as its final movement. Now he performed the entire oratorio in an evening concert. As in Dublin eight years earlier, the convergence of *Messiah* and a charitable cause produced a sensational response from the public, almost 1,400 people cramming the Hospital chapel where the performance was given. A tradition was born. Handel donated a

*Chapel, Foundling Hospital, by Thomas Rowlandson and Augustus Pugin for
Ackermann's* Microxosm of London *(1808-1811)*

Salisbury, Bristol (where it received its first hearing in a cathedral in 1758), Bath, Cambridge, Birmingham, Liverpool, Newcastle, and Derby. After 1767, when the full score was finally published and readily available, *Messiah* performances rapidly increased, and the oratorio took ship for performances in Europe and America.

copy of the conducting score, and each year thereafter until 1777 a charity performance of Messiah was given at the Foundling Hospital.

Handel personally conducted *Messiah* some thirty times. But during the second half of the Eighteenth Century, the oratorio increasingly found its way into concerts performed by others (at first, each one authorized by Handel). Appropriately, this began in Dublin, where the Charitable Musical Society gave annual performances of the oratorio from 1744. Over the next years it received performances in Oxford,

In 1784, two years before Susannah Cibber died and was buried in the cloister of Westminster Abbey (Handel is also buried there, in Poet's Corner), a grand "Commemoration of Handel" took place at the Abbey, featuring a *Messiah* performance with five hundred instrumentalists and singers, a portent of the oratorio's performance by even more gigantic forces in Nineteenth Century choral festivals. The money collected at the Commemoration went to the Fund for the Support of Decay'd Musicians.

In the Twenty-first Century *Messiah* finds itself among that tiny, illustrious handful of works that is perpetually in performance. Though it now most often finds itself nestled among the holly and ivy of Christmastime, it is also increasingly programmed during the Easter season in which it was first presented. And it is a safe bet that on any date of the calendar a production of *Messiah*, professional or amateur, is being planned, rehearsed, or performed.

Conceived in the nadir of a composer's career, born and nurtured in exile, and taking its first awkward steps through a storm of bigotry, *Messiah* has taken its place as an honored and evergreen immortal. Long may it do its work of bringing hope to the world. ❦

- Cambridge 2006

The Handel Monument in Westminster Abbey,
sculpture by Roubillac, engraving reproduced in the
British Printer, 1894, page 54

Silverleaf Press Books are available exclusively through Independent Publishers Group.

For details write or telephone Independent Publishers Group, 814 North Franklin St. Chicago, IL 60610, (312) 337-0747 Silverleaf Press 8160 South Highland Drive Sandy, Utah 84093

ISBN 13: 978-1-93439-305-5

Design by Amy Orton

Pictures on pages 9, 37, 38, 46, 61 courtsey of Handel House Museum, London Pictures on pages 44, 63, 71 courtsey of Mary Evans Photo Library, London

All other images from various surces and in public domain. Please contact Silverleaf with any questions or concerns concerning the use of imagery.